The Little Warrior

The Little Warrior

ALDIVAN TORRES

Canary Of Joy

CONTENTS

1

∽

"The Little Warrior"
    Aldivan Teixeira Torres
The Little Warrior

Author: Aldivan Teixeira Torres
© 2019-Aldivan Teixeira Torres
All rights reserved

Aldivan Teixeira Torres is a consolidated writer in several genres. To date, titles have been published in dozens of languages. From an early age, he was always a lover of the art of writing having consolidated a professional career from the second semester of 2013. He hopes with his writings to contribute to international culture, awakening the pleasure of reading in those who do not yet have the habit. Its mission is to win the hearts of each of its readers. In addition to literature, his main tastes are music, travel, friends, family, and the pleasure of living. "For literature, equality, fraternity, justice, dignity, and honor of the human being always" is his motto.

8-Pre-life

A spirit rests in the seventh heaven after long and intense material and immaterial lives. Among them, he participated with other spirits in the creation of the universe approximately fourteen billion years ago, helping beings created in their formation and development.

More recently, with the creation of the Earth, he was transferred here. Together with the six higher archangels, they organized a modern system of administration that aimed to establish the celestial kingdom. This situation put them in charge of billions of beings newly created by the supreme light.

Millions of years have passed in pure harmony. Until, out of pure pride, one of the archangels deviated from the norms of the greater father. He started a revolt on the celestial plane whose main objective was to take power only for himself.

The angels were divided into two fronts of battle, one favoring the black archangel and the other favoring light, the son of light and the remaining six archangels. The number of rebels was estimated at one third of the total.

In this battle, the greatest of all time, many lives were sacrificed for life and freedom. God only intruded when it gained an unexpected proportion (the angels had free will), threatening the support of the universe.

Then the supreme light set fire to the battlefield, separating the dissenting parties. With Miguel's help, the black archangel and his cronies were locked in the abyss (A dark, hot, horrible place) from which they could only leave with permission.

Then peace reigned. The spirit I am talking about has returned to its normal activities. He incarnated on earth several times as soon as material creation began. In these opportunities, he had the opportunity to evolve and teach concurrently.

At the right time, once again the cycle started again with the spirit called by light for yet another important mission on planet Earth. Its conception dates from October 17, 1982. Forward, warrior!

9-Birth

The day finally comes after nine months of expectation for the farming couple José Figueira Torres and Mary living in Leaf Village. As medical care was more highly regarded in the neighboring municipality, Arcoverde, Dona Maria was sent there.

During the thirty minutes of travel, in a car, a new jeep (Year 1980), lived the final moments of a risky pregnancy in the company of her husband. Even though she was afraid, she did everything to endure until she arrived at the hospital.

Luckily, he did it. They arrived in time. The car parked near the main entrance. The two went down. Maria, with a long dress without print, simple sandals, nails, and hair to be done. José wore shorts and shirt, leather hat and black shoes.

Assisted in walking by her husband, in five minutes they entered the hospital. as the case was urgent, Maria was promptly attended and sent to the delivery room. Meanwhile, José is accommodated in the waiting room.

José tries to distract himself in the best possible way between conversations, watching television, memories of past events to deceive nervousness and not think about the worst. He also takes the opportunity to analyze his role as a father since he got married until the respective moment. He concludes that he left a lot to be desired because he was very involved with work, prejudices, exaggerated rigidity and even hidden betrayals.

Would he be able to fix it, becoming a better father for this new son and for the four already grown up? Yes, he could, but for the time being it was not in his plans to change. He preferred to remain in ignorance and intolerance, a lesson he learned as a son in the forties.

It was a pity. It continues to be distracted. At one point, watch the clock. Three hours had passed and no response. Because he can't wait any longer, he gets up and goes to find one of the nurses at the hospital.

He finds one of them leaving the delivery room and hears a baby cry. It is reported that everything was fine with the wife and son. It was a boy.

Radiant with joy, he is allowed to enter the room. Upon entering it, seeing the figure of the wife with the child, she feels the same emotion or even greater than the other four times. He was rich in the graces of the Lord.

He comes closer, hugs his wife, picks up his son and cries. Quickly, she wipes her tears so as not to be embarrassed because she has learned that a man cannot cry in any situation.

After the moment, he returns the son to his wife and goes to see the doctors to release them. He is told that in the evening he could leave the hospital.

He stays with his wife again to take care of the baby. At 12:00 pm, lunch is served for both. An hour later, they are finally released. They leave the hospital, get in the car and start the journey back.

It would be another thirty minutes. Upon arriving home, the whole family would have the opportunity to meet the boy, who would be called Divine Torres, grandson of the legendary Victor Torres.

Let's move forward.

10-The first five years

In this period, like any normal child, Divine Torres gradually overcame the early stages of life. In the beginning, it depended on everyone for everything. But as the days and months went by, he started to get firmer, to sit, to crawl, to pronounce the first words and to become aware of the world around him.

When he was three years old, he was enrolled in the school to have contact with the first letters. I studied in the morning. This fact was important because from then on, he started to socialize more with children of his age and with adults of different mentality, something until then new.

From the age of four, he began to have a greater sense of the various aspects of life. As expected, doubts began to arise, and he used every moment to ask adults, especially parents. However, the answers did not always satisfy him.

At the age of five, she lost her grandfather as a mother, leaving only the two grandmothers. However, there was no dimension to the meaning of death. He attended the funeral just for attending.

From then on, with the brain more developed, the memories started to become stronger and the experiences that followed would be marked forever. Keep watching carefully, readers.

11-The vampire

After a day of intense activity, the night came, and it was not long before the full moon filled the sky with the peaceful Leaf Village. On this day, Divine Torres completed exactly five years and six months. As part of an ancient line of visionaries, the astral set this date for a frightening and spectacular event for his beginner's life.

He, together with his family, lived in a simple house style, narrow (five meters) and long (fifteen meters). It had a wooded entrance and a high wall, whose construction date was from the end of the 19th century. It was their second home.

Known as a haunted house, all the former residents either ran out of there or died tragically. But these aspects did not scare the Torres family, who preferred to think it was just rumors.

That same night, Divine, was put to sleep as usual in his simple crib, next to his parents' room. At the end of the prayers, the light was turned off. When the boy relaxed to sleep, instantly that lasted a fraction of a second, the figure of a terrifying man appeared howling and showing his claws and grown teeth.

With a start, Divine gave a loud cry and the vision disappeared. It was his first spiritual experience, which demonstrated that he was the one chosen to inherit extrasensory gifts. And now? Was he prepared to face the consequences of fate? Only time would have answers to these questions, and it was too early to worry about that. After all, he wasn't even six years old.

12- Other facts of this year (1989)

12.1-Accidents

Divine was a quiet boy, but like any child when he mixed with others, he practiced pranks. At some of these times, without a sense of danger he was involved in some accidents. Among them, it is worth mentioning: Burning with a boiling pan, cuts revolving garbage, butchers involving playing with sheep, beating for mischief.

However, although painful, each of these events left him a lesson which he strove to avoid next time. As the saying goes, knowledge heals and saves.

12.2-Spiritual facts

As previously said, the house in which Divine resided was haunted and the spirits that inhabited it began to use their dark forces to expel those they considered visitors.

The night was the preferred time for demonstrations. The most common ones were: Strong footsteps throughout the hallway of the house, the sound of breaking glasses and plates, people blowing on the coal and wood fire, the appearance of spirits dressed in their shroud, torches of light illuminating the whole house, knocking on bedroom doors.

However, not everyone understood the facts as this required a little sensitivity. But the house was proven to be haunted. Each day, Divine expanded his range of knowledge even though he did not yet have a dimension of his infinite powers.

12.3-Social facts

Even this year, Divine increased its social circle and was already very popular throughout the village. He had learned to read and write, did school activities at friends' houses, participated in school celebrations, played, swam, knew the undergrowth around the house, climbed the mountain and went to help his parents in the fields. He had given his first unpretentious kiss and at the end of the year he had finished preschool.

All these steps were important for self-knowledge, helping you to have a place in society and in everyone's heart. Forward, Divine!

13-The year of change

1990. In the last year, Divine had grown as never. He had evolved physically, intellectually and morally and was now ready for new constructive, enriching and challenging experiences. Gradually, he understood his gift better and talked openly with his family about it.

It was there that they told him a little about the story of his grandfather, the legendary Victor. This left him from relieved to content. Now, he didn't feel like a stranger in the world. Someone had already been through something similar even though they hadn't met him.

According to the need, his father, José Torres, was teaching him some things about the spiritual side. For the respect he had, Divine listened to him attentively. However, not everything could yet understand.

Only one thing was obvious: There was a division in the universe between two balanced forces and that because he had an incredible gift it was up to him to fulfill a great mission on Earth. But his time had not yet come.

Meanwhile, as a boy, it was up to Divine to take advantage of this phase of life to learn, teach and play. Anyway, be a child like any other. The responsibilities would only come in adulthood.

Regarding family-social interactions, everything happened within the normal range. Just a novelty: His family had decided to move again. This time, to the main site of the site that was going to be renovated and electricity was made available for it.

The renovation began in August. As the family did not have many financial conditions, everything was ready only at the end of October of the same year. On the very second of November, the change containing the small pieces of furniture was carried out.

From that day on, a new phase began. Now, they were far from the influence of the haunting of the previous house. Would they be happy? What new challenges would arise in the life of that blessed family? Nobody knew, but it was also in the blood of modern Torres to fight and dedicate themselves to their projects following the example of the brothers Rafael and Victor.

Keep going always.

14-The 1991-1997 period

Life went on. Divine continued to evolve in every way. An intelligent boy, he dedicated himself very hard to studies at school and at home where he spent most of his time because he had a very homely, almost antisocial, education. This type of education chosen by parents had advantages and disadvantages. Among the advantages, he was involved in fewer fights and accidents. Regarding disadvantages, he missed the opportunity to get to know the surrounding people more deeply with different points of view, thus making relationships and friendships more difficult. Solitude sometimes hit hard also between the four walls in which he was accustomed to living at least ten hours a day.

Regarding the spiritual part, he periodically had new experiences that strengthened his contact with beings from other planes. Among the most striking were the appearance of a vampire under the bed, a man watching him as he slept and premonitory and enlightening dreams.

It can be seen from the text that nothing was yet clear or defined in his life. Divine had already turned fourteen, completed high school and would be enrolled in high school the following year. He was going to study at the Pesqueira headquarters.

15-The farewell (1998)

The year begins. Religious celebrations take place in the village and finally the school calendar begins. From the first day, Divine Torres was willing to learn and teach in his new school stronghold that included high school and elementary school.

The college was located almost in the center of Pesqueira. It was a large, spacious building with three floors overlapping. It was the biggest Divine had ever known in his short, but mysterious, intriguing and passionate life.

There, he had contact with the principals, employees and new classmates and schoolmates. He was well-received by everyone despite his great shyness that made relationships difficult. However, because he is from the rural area, he felt a little prejudice. But I didn't know if this was just an impression.

One, two, almost three months passed. He felt more in touch with everyone and continually stood out on his study mornings. In one of these, one of the directors came into the room, called him out and when he was away from his colleagues he started babbling:

"Look, Divine, your father is not doing well, and we heard that he got worse.

At that moment, the boy noticed something in the director's voice and sensed that that was not the whole truth. With a little fear and even courage, he asked:

"He died?

"Yea. How does it feel?

"I do not know.

"Look, someone came to pick you up to accompany you to the funeral. You can go, you're excused from classes today. It's out there.

"Thanks.

The young man walked away from the principal and took a few steps toward the exit. Soon, I was already descending the steps of the stairs. With each step, he felt a weight on his body and spirit that he could not explain. Why was fate repeated? What would happen to him and his family? He would have to learn to live with this new reality and conform because it was part of his Maktub, something that nobody could avoid or change.

Divine continues down the stairs and as she approached the end, she has the slight feeling that she is not alone. With that, he feels more secure, quickens his pace and finally reaches the first floor. Go through the door and the person are waiting.

This is Alberto, one of his neighbors who kindly came to pick him up by car at the request of his mother, Mary. After greeting him, the two get into the car and Alberto starts the game.

Realizing the teenager's sadness, Alberto communicates little for respect. He only does it out of compassion, about halfway through the stretch.

"I am very sorry for the loss of your father. He was a good man. Hardworking, dignified and honest.

"Thanks. Today it was him. Another day will be us. This is life.

"I admire your attitude. If it were another, he would be dying to scream.

"What's the use? We humans must at least accept God's designs. This is what we have left.

"I agree. How painful that is. I say this from experience.

"Know. You already lost your wife. What I can say is that she is happy where she is.

"As you know?

"I intuition at this moment of great sensitivity.

"Thank you for the words.

Alberto accelerated and tried to be quiet. Talking about his wife brought up old wounds not yet healed. It was best not to remember. From then on, silence prevails until arriving at Leaf Village, specifically at Divine's house.

The car stopped. The little dreamer came down, said goodbye and without looking back ran into the house. Upon entering, he greeted some people and found his mother desolate in the kitchen. At the meeting, the two hugged and moaning softly his mother said:

"God took him, son!

"And now? What will become of us? (Divine)

"Financially nothing will change because I will keep the pension, but this is the least important thing now. (Maria)

"At least I still have you. (Divine)

Tears came down from both of their faces, further increasing their empathy. From now on, Maria would be the mainstay of the house, and it was up to the children to follow her obediently.

Five minutes later, the hug ceased, and they felt more relaxed. Each went about his business. While Maria went to pay attention to the visitors, her son entered a room and sat desolate in one of the beds. The moment reflected the sadness of him, his family and relatives, friends and neighbors.

In this funeral mood, the morning passed. Nobody in the house tasted food at lunchtime by making just a snack. The afternoon started and other people arrived for the funeral, increasing the movement in the house.

Around 4:00 pm, the train finally left for the local cemetery. Five strong men offered to carry the coffin while the others followed closely. They crossed the entire village, took the dirt road facing the sun, the dust and the hard and dry ground.

Throughout the journey, many remembered the main achievements of that sinful, but dignified and honest man. This generous attitude brought a little spiritual relief to family members who were in great need of comfort.

With another fifteen minutes of walking, they finally arrive at the cemetery. The doors are opened and the train has access along with the rest of the crowd. The coffin is gently lowered into the grave and the last tributes are paid to José Torres, son of the legendary Victor Torres.

The coffin hits land, and they start throwing dirt into the hole until it is completely covered. After this operation, they were all dismissed and would go on with their lives.

This was a natural fact that should be followed by everyone, especially for those involved in the matter. Of the deceased, good memories would remain in the minds of those who loved him despite his numerous shortcomings.

Always moving forward, living life without being ashamed of being happy!

16-transition process

After his death, José Torres' soul did not immediately reach peace because of his countless landslides. In disembodiment, he was taken by angels' followers of Satan who led him to limbo, an intermediate place.

However, it was not abandoned by God who gave him a possibility of salvation: Finding someone pure, close to God, who would sacrifice for him. If he succeeded, he would at least achieve purification in purgatory.

It was there that a great journey began for him. Once a month, I was allowed to go back to earth and try to find this person. During these wanderings, he ended up choosing his son, Divine, as he was closer, pure, and well-connected to his religion.

She met him about seven times between visions and dreams. At the last, he made the sacrifice request. Due to the little experience, he had, the boy did not understand well, but for him to believe that the experience was real, a hand touched him after he woke up from the dream. This caused him a mixture of fear and anxiety. However, I would try to help.

The other day, he fulfilled the request even amid protests from his family. He did not speak up because everything was a big secret. At the end of the afternoon, he ended his work. Mission Accomplished.

A few days after the sacrifice, he had the expected response. His father came to say goodbye to him definitively because he had reached God's forgiveness with his help.

This moment was of great emotion for the two, assisted by a powerful angel. Divine was unable to see him because of his glory, but he can see his light and his flapping wings. Moments later, they left.

Joseph was to begin his cycle of evolution in the spiritual realm and would rarely return to earth. It was the beginning of a great journey, a real crossing, and he would have to do it away from everyone.

The sprout of the inland would continue his life together with his family on Earth. There was still a lot to accomplish.

17-The period of (1999-2000)

Life went on normally for Divine and her family. Over time, the memories of the deceased became less painful and shocking. This fact was absolutely normal. After all, what has passed. What mattered was the gift that was still challenging for everyone.

The Torres family was a quiet, humble family, earning two minimum wages distributed to six people with well-defined moral and ethical values. However, not everyone shared the same opinions, preferences, tastes, and education. What united them was the sacred blood of the seers, formed by Jewish, Portuguese, Spanish, indigenous and Gypsy descent.

All were dedicated to agriculture and did not try or have the opportunity to study. The exception to the Matriarch Mary, who was retired and took care of the house and the young Divine, who devoted himself entirely to his studies. The names of the other children were Absalão, Adeildo, José Amaro and Bianca.

As can be seen, Divine was the only hope for financial improvement because only education is capable of transforming a reality and performing miracles. The same, despite his young age, was fully aware of this.

In this way, he studied changing schools a couple of times. He met new people, interacted, but still with reservations wrapped in his prejudices. He didn't even know that he was wasting precious time in his life.

The problem with that young man, raised in a Catholic tradition, was that he took her religion and laws very literally (many still do the same thing today). For him, anything took the notion of sin as parties, walks and even sex (don't laugh).

He was truly an eccentric. He lived a simple life, full of rules that only hindered him instead of helping. But I didn't see it at any time. In this regard, the grandfather who had lived at the beginning of the 20th century had given himself up early to the emotions that life provided.

Even following this line, this did not prevent him from experiencing strong emotions. He lived the experience of passion intensely without even realizing it for the second time. In the first, he had been rejected and in the second he had not even tried. He preferred to suffer in secret for a long time. Until on a certain day, the person realized his intention and gave him a massive out. Another disappointment occurred. He was beginning to experience this face of love which, in my opinion, is very constructive despite being painful.

Over time, he managed to overcome. He continued his studies normally. At the end of 2000, he finished high school. Now a new stage in his life was beginning.

18-New course (2001-2002)

The year 2000 ends. 2001 begins with great news. Among them, the most important were Divine's two approvals in selection processes (the result of his efforts). One related to a public tender and the other was the entry into a federal technical course (electromechanical specialty).

When February came, classes started after an intense family vacation (the only option because I didn't have the money to travel). From the beginning, Divine loved the environment: a large, wooded space composed of several blocks and very heterogeneous classmates, with people of various age groups, ethnicities and social classes.

Throughout the time, the young man devoted himself intensively to his studies without neglecting the friendships that were also important to him. In a time of little money, he lived to borrow books for his colleagues, to take dangerous rides with another colleague in his region and to always wear his uniform because he had no choice of clothes. However, I still had the same big and pure heart as always and that was what really mattered.

And so, time went on with Divine's life centered on studies. Near the end of the course, in November 2002, a meeting was organized at the school to find out who would be interested in competing for the first internship vacancies whose test would take place at the beginning of the next month in a nearby city called Garanhuns. At that moment, the little dreamer felt for the first time a suffocating and screaming force that drove him to drop everything. Even if they tried to resist, the pressure increased every moment. If he didn't decide, it would explode. It was there that he approached the course coordinator and said:

"I will not go.

From then on, I was aware that I had left all the work of two years behind and had no way of communicating with anyone who could help because I had no cell phone or computer. Everything went downhill and the dream of helping the family became more distant, although he was waiting for the nomination in a public contest.

Let's move forward.

19- Farewell trip

19.1-First day

After the theoretical classes of the course in question were concluded, someone gave the idea of organizing a trip where everyone could enjoy a lot and say goodbye because each one would take a different course and probably would not meet again.

The location chosen was the Xingó plant, on the border between Alagoas and Sergipe. This time, Divine would go. After all, it was a unique opportunity to get to know this giant of the national hydroelectric complex, nearby cities and to strengthen ties with colleagues. It would literally be a farewell.

On the scheduled day and time, with his suitcase ready, he waited on the track next to his village (at the side of Highway BR 232) for the bus. Three hours passed and nothing. Anguished and disgusted, he decided to return to his home.

Arriving at the same time, he went to his bed and went to try to sleep. When he managed to relax, he had the long-awaited rest. Around 6:00 am, he woke with a start with voices calling his name on the door.

When he went out to check, he realized that it was his classmates who came to call him for the trip, and he was frightened by it. I thought they were gone a long time ago. He was convinced to go again, said goodbye to his family, got on the bus and finally left for Xingó.

The bus started following inland, passing through the city never seen by the boy. How big the world was! It was a pleasure to discover this little by little.

In a total of approximately three and a half hours of travel, with much excitement for the passengers, they arrived in the city of Piranhas (specifically to the accommodation). They unpacked their bags and rested for a while. It would be two days of intense experiences for everyone away from the family and their private worlds.

After lunch, the first activity to take place: The visit to the Xingó hydroelectric plant, one of the main reasons for the trip. Some did not want to go, but those who did have a unique experience.

The difficult-to-reach place, a narrow, winding road, impressed Divine. I had never seen it like this. Despite the fear, the taste for adventure was greater. At the end of the road, he had a view of part of the dam and the floodgates. Amazing! A fantastic piece of engineering! It wouldn't be the same after this.

Just ahead, they had access to the entrance. They took the elevator down to the basement. Once there, they could closely observe the complex devices that were part of the plant. The noise of the turbines was constant, as well as the tremor. The nature that produced it was a force that had to be respected. Lesson number one from the trip.

In thirty minutes, they understood the energy reality a little more closely, giving real bases to the theoretical part learned in the course. At the end of this period, they said goodbye and took the elevator up again. They reach normal altitude. They returned to the bus.

As it was almost night, they went to the center of Piranhas to find a quiet place to have dinner and talk for a while.

In twenty minutes, they found a typical restaurant and the class split into tables. Some ordered traditional food (rice, beans, meat) while others ordered something different, cassava with beef jerky (Divine and her table friends).

They waited for a while. Moments later, the food was served. While they ate, they chatted away about school moments, the city, the trip and personal aspects.

It was fifteen minutes of intense exchange of information and great pleasure with the tasting of local spices. After dinner, they returned to the bus that headed for the accommodation.

Once there, it was just time to take a shower and change clothes.

Divine and his friends left again. This time on foot, to get to know a little of the night.

Without much experience, the group was walking for a long time until they found a nice place by indication of places. It was a show house. Arriving at the same and met at a table (there were four in total). In sequence, they asked for something to drink and were just talking.

They waited a few moments. The drink arrived, and they took a few sips (except Divine who didn't drink). The music started, and then they took the courage to invite some kittens sitting at the next table.

Invitation accepted, the four together with their partners went to the ballroom and started to dance to romantic music on the night of Alagoas.

How good this moment was! The combination of the music and the girls' grace awoke a kind of trance in them that seemed to be completed with each step taken. It was really incredible!

Nothing but the music or the steps mattered to them. They were experiencing a kind of freedom, far from the envious looks of enemies, spite, and even pressure from family members.

It was very healthy. After an hour of fun, they got tired and invited the girls to stay by their table. Again, they accepted.

For the next two hours, they talked with each other and between two couples there was chemistry. Kisses and hugs rolled at night. After this period, the visitors said goodbye, and together they started their way back to the accommodation.

Of the girls, only the memory would remain because none of them intended to have a serious relationship with anyone. After all, they were too young for that.

Thirty minutes later, they reached the goal. They went to their rooms, fell on the bed and tried to relax. The other day would have to be enjoyed to the fullest as it was the last one in that interesting and hospitable city.

19.2- The second day

It dawns in the beautiful and pleasant Piranhas. Since early morning, the students of University of Pesqueira were engaged in the kitchen preparing breakfast after a quick shower. As there was not much choice, breakfast would be the basics: bread with eggs and coffee.

In twelve minutes, everything was ready and the snack was distributed equally among all. Between conversations and laughter, this moment passed rapidly. At the end, everyone returned to their rooms to get ready (including suitcases) for one last walk.

In about another fifteen minutes, everyone had completed this work. They then met and as they saw that no one was missing, they went to the bus. First destination: São Francisco River banks.

With good speed, it didn't take long for everyone to arrive with a lot of excitement. The bus stopped. They had thirty minutes to enjoy the beach. Descending one by one, each one made the most of this time in the best possible way: taking photos, diving, sunbathing and admiring the beautiful landscape.

In the case of Divine, only the last two items as he did not have a camera or knew how to swim. But even so, it was very worthwhile to participate with colleagues in such incredible and unforgettable moments.

After their time, they returned to the bus and left for destination 2: Archaeological Museum in the neighboring city called Canindé de São Francisco, which was approximately six kilometers from the place where they were.

On this quick journey, the young man took the opportunity to relax and think a little about everything he had left behind: The family, his little Leaf Village, his friends and acquaintances. Despite the longing, he concluded that everything had been very worthwhile. When could I go out again? I didn't even have a project. So, the time to take advantage was now.

It was with this disposition that he quickly left the vehicle when it arrived and stopped at the indicated place. Together with the others, he paid the entrance fee and entered the imposing building of the Xingó Archaeological Museum in the city of Canindé de São Francisco.

Inside it, visitors had the opportunity to discover ancient artifacts, bones of nomads and ancient inhabitants, giving them an overview of the prehistory of the place. The tour was excellent.

After passing through all sectors, having taken many pictures and having learned a lot, the group finally headed for the exit. Passing the gate, they headed back to the bus.

With a few more steps, they board the vehicle. They settle down and the driver starts. Destination 3: Home with a probable stop for lunch on the way.

They pass through some localities and arriving close to 12:00 o'clock they stop at a gas station by the road. Everyone then descends, walks a little, enters the establishment and gets in a line to eat because the restaurant operated in self-service mode.

When they have access to the shelves, each one will place their preferred food and settle on the available tables. Some ask for something to drink like juice or soda.

Between meal, chat and rest, another thirty minutes pass. When everyone is finished, the group pays for the meal and returns to the bus. They had a long way to go.

In the remaining two and a half hours, mostly silent, Divine, and her colleagues prefer to relax as much as they can. In the evening, they arrive in Arcoverde, and there is a quick stop. Fifteen minutes to satisfy physiological needs. Then, go back to the road.

With a few more minutes, they finally reach Leaf Village. Divine says goodbye and comes down with his heavy suitcase. In a matter of minutes, he would arrive at his residence. Now, he would have to walk his path, and he did not know what fate had in store.

What he knew was that he would continue to fight for his goals and even if he delayed, he believed he would win. Onward, warrior! Whatever is written, will happen!

20-The new reality

Finished the cycle of studies at University of Pesqueira, Divine Torres enrolled in a computer course with the objective of not standing still beside studying for competitions and waiting for the call in the competition in which he was approved in a good position.

Despite being always active, his situation was not good because the goals he pursued were not yet attainable his hand and how painful this wait was. He felt somewhat powerless for not helping his needy family.

However, at the moment there was nothing to do. The conditions were terrible and no one known was willing to help to show how selfish the world was. Even so, I wouldn't give up easily.

And life went on ....

21-Six months later

A long time passed and Divine's situation had not yet changed: She was still studying computer science and studying at home. As for the contest in which he expected to be called, the expiration date had ended, ending there with his hopes.

From then on, the demotivation had hit hard. As a consequence, there was a disconnection from reality making the spiritual part become stronger. With that, his knowledge increased from really impressive experiences.

The lineage of the seer blood screamed within itself the fruit of an inheritance left by the grandfather, the legendary Victor.

22-Experiences

22.1-Possession

It was a normal Wednesday. After the normal obligation to study at home in the morning and lunch, Divine entered her room to rest for a while in her bed, the famous siesta. After taking off his striped T-shirt and Jeans shorts, he lay down comfortably talking.

He concentrated on leaving his mind clear and gradually relaxed. Something fantastic happened! Suddenly, a round white object descended on him and entered his head.

From that day on, his life changed completely. He started to have more real contacts with beings from other dimensions, feeling his presence and what is impressive having struggles with them using the powers acquired with the possession.

With each passing moment, his powers increased further, increasing his pride a little. However, the situation did not last long in these terms.

He also started to attract powerful spirits who started to take advantage in the fights and what is worse, the spirit that dominated him used his body as a shield. It was no longer an advantage for Divine in this kind of situation.

That's when someone helped him. Your deceased father. He approached, crossed his arms and with great effort expelled the inconvenient spirit. Fortunately! Divine was now free from possession and one hand washes the other. Blessed father!

However, there was much to learn about the spiritual side.

22.2-Postmortem: Dispute for souls

Another interesting fact was the revelation of the struggle of the two opposing forces (the existing duality) when people die.

It was more or less the following: Raquel and Romero Bastos, newly separated from the matter were a little lost in an intermediate zone between the Earth and the spiritual planes characterized by without a vast field, without ground, sky and a little dark. At this moment, the two still did not understand what had happened.

That was when a big shadow approached them with screams of horror and sarcasm.

On the other hand, distantly, a light came on. The two were confused and asked:

"What is happening? What is this shadow and light?

"Telepathically, someone said: The shadow is the head of the Rebel Angels and the light an angel of God.

It was there that the black Archangel came closer and revealed his shape, making them even more astonished.

"Wow, how big he is. It is a giant before us! (Raquel and Romero exclaimed in amazement)

Before the Angel arrived, Satan approached them, grabbed them in his hands and said: You are all mine!

At this moment, she hears a great cry for help and mercy from them and Raquel said:

"You cannot do more than God!

Satan, with his usual sarcasm, replied:

"It is true! But where is this God? It takes faith and you don't have it.

With this response, it was Romero's turn to speak up:

"You have no right to take me. I never stole, killed or did injustice. I'm good. We are children of God!

This complaint was the key piece for the light to manifest. Then more angels appeared, surrounded Satan and drove him away. The devil really had no right to torment Raquel and Romero, who were good people in life. As Jesus promised, the light belongs to the righteous.

However, if it were the case of people distorted, Satan would be allowed to take them and torment them as much as he wanted. For each one reaps what he sows in the barn (which is this world) and God is also Justice! Just the reminder. Wake up, people! Let go of grudge, selfishness, pride, intrigue and always do good without looking at whom. We never know when our day will be.

Obs.:(Real Facts).

22.30- Postmortem: The bitter price of a soul

God's mercy is very great when he is willing to save all his children, even the most sinful. The means for this miracle to take place is through his disciples on Earth, those who are willing to pay a certain price for the freedom of these souls.

Divine was one of those chosen for this type of work, having sacrificed himself several times for his brothers. However, in the last, he regretted being so good (the price of the soul was costly).

The price was to be beaten by the black archangel for an entire night. He suffered physically and morally from the offenses handed down. Among them, the main ones were:

"You took another soul from me. Who do you think you are? Do you want to be God? Do not meddle in matters that do not concern you.

At another point, the archangel continued:

"Look, if you take another soul from me, I will kill you boy, I will kill you! I just don't do it now because I'm not authorized.

In conclusion, he said:

"You felt sorry for that depraved and filthy soul. Tell me now: Who's taking pity on you? Sacrificing yourself for a God you don't even know.

In these moments of agony, Divine was comforted by the angels:

"Golden boy, that's why God loves you so much. (Gabriel)

"You will receive endless blessings, and you will become a great man. (Miguel)

"All the good you do on Earth; you will receive twice as much reward in heaven. (Rafael)

The ordeal took a while longer and, in the end, Divine was at peace. I wasn't convinced if I wanted to repeat the experience, but I was happy for the souls I had helped to save.

Moral of the story: Donating is a courageous attitude that only true friends do. Prefer them to the money, power, vanity, and ostentation that are passengers.

22.4-Encounter with God

At one point, Divine was wandering around meeting several people along the way. With each good deed, he did towards these people, his inner light increased, smothering the surrounding darkness that put him in danger.

There comes a time when the light intensifies a lot and the darkness moves away completely. At the end of the path, a mysterious voice spoke to him: "You are the light of the lights, the true light of the world.

That said, the route was completed successfully.

Moral of the story: Make a difference. Choose the light. Transform the world with your ideas. Practice charity, love, and detachment. Also be a child of light as Divine is.

22.5-The authority of God

Divine's gift developed visibly, but there was total lack of control over him. He attracted low-vibration spirits who took pleasure in harassing him, making him almost mad. It was then that one of these times God intervened:

"Obsessive spirits, stay away from this young man.

The spirits replied:

"We are not going away. We will continue to hurt him because it gives us pleasure.

Divine's spiritual guide who was always by his side also took part:

"Get away from him. Obey God. Otherwise, everyone will go to hell.

"We don't obey anyone. (Obsessing spirits)

God then manifested himself again:

"Very well. They will regret that they challenged me. You should destroy them. However, I have a better punishment. Lucifer, come here.

Promptly, a shadow approached in obedience to the creator and came close to Divine and the possessors. He asked by the light:

"Yes, master, I am here. What do you wish?

"Take these spirits with you. I don't want them anymore.

"As you wish.

"Look, be careful not to hurt the boy.

Lucifer then started to grab them one by one.

The obsessed, frightened and angry spirits cried out:

"You pay us, we will take revenge.

Lucifer interrupted:

"There is no point in threatening him. I, who am a God, cannot do anything against him. How much more, you.

When Lucifer took possession of everyone, the supreme light again manifested itself:

"Ready. You can withdraw.

"It's ok. When you want to give me more souls, just call me.

That said, Lucifer withdrew with the spirits and with that Divine became calmer. The evil had been removed.

Moral of the story: Pray and always watch brothers because evil is everywhere and our defense is our faith. In case of distress, turn to the Lord of hosts that he will understand you.

22.6-The importance of man in God's plan

We are the culmination of creation, the reflection of the creator, the meaning of life. We were created to dream, evolve, live and love. Each person represents a piece of divinity. We are immersed in everything, which represents the living soul of this planet.

To illustrate, I will tell you two important facts in Divine's life:

1. The encounter with Miguel: As we know, after giving up on the course, Divine was experiencing a very intense spiritual conflict.

It was as if good and evil were fighting within each other. It was there that, in despair, he invoked the presence of Miguel Archangel and for having a pure soul God granted the asking, sending him. It was a clear night, with low temperature and to some extent calm. The apparition took place outside his house, when Divine went out to contemplate the stars (he felt a strong, intense light, something frightening by the intensity). Soon after his arrival, Divine felt better and instantly something prompted him to say the following: "You already saved me, you can go. For Jesus! At first, he did not obey (after all he is Miguel Archangel, one of the seven spirits of God). However, at Divine's insistence he ended up obeying and withdrew to his place of origin.

2. Divine had also entered a depressive crisis and had more and more difficulties sleeping. Then he started taking medicine. Tired of this subterfuge, one day, he decided that he would not take medicine and hopefully hoped to sleep. To this end, he prayed all night and at dawn he had the answer he expected. An angel came and touched him. From then on, he did not need to take any more medication.

Moral of the story: We are kings and lords even over angels and consistent faith can work miracles.

22.7- Extra corporeal experience

Many people in the world have already revealed that they have had cardiopulmonary experiences, especially NDE (near-death experience). On these occasions, some went to heaven, hell, limbo, or even the city of men.

In the case of Divine, it was spontaneous. As a result of fate, his spirit has become detached from the flesh and at this moment he can observe his body by the bed. Soon afterwards, assisted by his spiritual guide, he had a private meeting with a relative of his who had passed away. In this exciting encounter, he had the rare opportunity to chat, quench his thirst and spend good energy for a short time.

At the farewell, he gave his relative a big hug and kiss. Finally, he walked away, returning to the body thanks to his guide. The other day, he thanked his spiritual father for the rare and incredible blessing he had had.

He was really blessed.

22.8-Experience beyond time

Divine's spiritual powers were clearly growing. At one point, he managed to cross the timeline by transporting himself to the past. He returned to the forties, exactly at the place of his residence.

It was the date of its inauguration. Divine approached the hosts asking for permission to enter. He was kindly received by them and made a point of showing the houseroom by room: the cement was reddish in tone, curtains from side to side, well-designed rooms, but not very spacious, decorated with wooden furniture and religious paintings, a clean, prepared house and as it was night, the lamps were lit.

For several hours, Divine enjoyed this moment with very blessed people. In the end, he said goodbye, headed for the exit and had already made the trip back to his time. Another incredible fact in your life!

Moral of the story: There is nothing impossible for those who believe in God, that is, in the benign forces of the universe.

22.9-Spiritual healing

It is a process in which the psychic medium incorporates a spirit capable of assisting him in operations that can result in the cure of the sick person's disease.

On this topic, Divine had the following experience: He was invited to observe the operation of a boy who had a brain tumor. With great delicacy, Doctor Ramei, assisted by nurse Cristina, took care of all the stages of this process. At the end of the procedure, the tumor disintegrated. Thanks, and glories to those who did only good!

The power of healing

Once upon a time, a paraplegic by birth was called Giliard. As was natural, his life was not at all easy and despite his faith in God he sometimes wondered what sin he would have committed to suffer so much. His dream was to walk again.

To get around, he used a wheelchair that he himself drove. He used it all the time, even on the streets. It was there that one day a disgrace occurred. Crossing a busy avenue, he was surprised by a runaway car that crashed into it. The impact was brutal, causing his death.

Already dead, he remained with the same difficulties. At this moment, he had the opportunity to meet his angel, whose name was Balzak. This divine envoy, full of mercy, decided to help him.

She carried him in her arms and took him to the Young Divine. She placed him beside her, next to the bed and said:

"Touch it and you will be healed.

Giliard, moved by an impressive internal force, repeated the following in thought:

"Even if I touch only his fingertip, I will be healed.

With some effort, his fingers touched Divine's body and, in that instant, a force came out of the young man and healed him. Initially, he was a little staggered, but little by little he was steadying his feet and he was erect. Glory to God! (Exclaimed the same)

He met with his angel and let himself be carried away. Now he was healed and could go in peace and without resentment to the kingdom of light.

Moral of the story: Faith produces true miracles.

22.10- The attack of the demons

Divine's process of evolution continued between light and darkness. On a day when he was unprepared, that is, with his body open, the demons were allowed to approach him. There were about ten of them, with their shiny wings, terrifying, animal-shaped shadows. I will transcribe some lines from this passage:

"I love to torment people like you, nice girls. (One spoke)

"We will enjoy that he is weak. (Other)

At this point, Divine's protector approached and scolded them:

"Stop harassing him, you unfortunates.

"Stop? Who's going to stop us? You? (One of them)

"If necessary, yes. (Divine Angel)

"We are outnumbered, bully. (Observed another)

Divine's angel seeing himself with his hands tied threatened:

"If you don't go out, I'll call one of the supreme princes to teach you a lesson.

"Who? Rafael? Gabriel? Miguel? I have bad memories of the last beating I took from them. They have the same strength as our God. (Commented the chief, denoting fear)

"Where's your boss? (Divine Angel)

"It is carrying souls in Asia. That's why he didn't come to have fun. (Informed)

The demons remained in their attack on Divine mercilessly. Full of commotion, the angel of the same manifested itself again:

"He arrives. I can't stand to see this massacre anymore.

"You are going to have to take it. We are a legion of powers while you are just a throne. (the boss)

At this moment, something mysterious and fantastic happened: A mysterious light emanated from Divine's body illuminating everyone around him. This fact removed the shadows of the demons who were forced to retreat.

Even if they were upset, they were forced to leave for good. Then Divine's angel came closer, embraced his protégé and commented:

"Calm. Everything will be fine now.

"Why do you torment me? (Wanted to know Divine)

"You are a rock in their shoe. Its mission is to bring people closer to God, definitively ending the cycle of darkness in this world. (Explained)

"Can I count on your help?

"Ever. In good times and bad, I will be with you. Now rest and sleep. Tomorrow is another day. A good night.

"Good night.

With the angel beside him, Divine relaxed and let himself be carried away. How long would you suffer? He hoped that this phase would pass soon and at the last moment would come.

Onward, warrior!

22.11-The angel and the messenger

Anyone has two distinct spiritual beings: an angel and a messenger. With her powers in development, Divine had contact with the two.

While one encouraged him, the other discouraged him, by forming his "Two opposites".

The following is an interesting experience of the same with these two entities.

A beautiful dark night with a full moon, the messenger approached close to 24:00. He sat on his bed and started chatting with Divine.

"Do you mean that you are the one who calls yourself the son of God?

"Yea. All men who follow divine law and open their minds to the light can be called "Children of God".

"You fool! You are not the son of God! I will prove it now.

That said, he leaned on one foot and with the other tried to crush the protégé with great anger. However, the movement of the foot did not end by being suspended in the air. It was there that his angel approached and came shouting:

"What do you want with my protégé?

"Just lower his crest.

"Monster! You don't have that right.

At this moment, a titanic fight between the two began using swords, shields, rays and stellar arrows. By fate, the angel took advantage and drove the messenger away.

With the mission accomplished, he approached Divine resting on his bed. In the next moment, she covered it with the palm of her hand. Thrilled, he exclaimed:

"If you didn't exist, I wouldn't exist either.

"Thank you, I love you too! (Returned Divine)

The rest of the night the little dreamer tried to rest while his angel was always on guard. Divine was truly a special being as he was one of the few on planet Earth who knew his angel. I could feel it and hear it. It was his link with the spiritual plane, with the divine. I hoped it would go on like this for a lifetime.

22.12-The weigher

On another day of spiritual weakness, a demon known as a heavy bar managed to get close to Divine. With his scarlet shadow and wings, he sat on the bed and gradually climbed on Divine's body.

Responding to this attack, Divine tried to transfigure himself to suffocate his darkness. However, this method did not work because its luminous halo had disappeared completely for an unknown reason.

Seeing Divine's effort, the demon exclaimed:

"You have a lot of power. However, he does not know how to use it correctly.

Without more barriers, the weigher climbed higher on Divine's body. When he completely mastered it, he communicated:

"I will suck up all of your vital energy!

Desperate, Divine made one last attempt to save himself: He thought of the image of Christ being flogged and crucified for his help. Immediately, the demon stirred and fled his presence.

Christ's blood really has power!

23-Secrets

23.1-The pressure of the earth

In addition to the increasingly fantastic spiritual discoveries, Divine experiences a corporeal-spiritual dilemma. I explain. As Divine was already in an advanced stage of evolution, she refused to have sex to do. For him, sex was a complement to a healthy relationship that he had not yet found. With this, his material body pressed him more and more causing physical problems.

It was there that God manifested himself through the Virgin Mary. She was kneeling in the skies asking her son for him:

""My son, look out for that creature. You who are so powerful and beneficial, heal him.

"Not my mom. The time has not come to heal him. Besides, I made a deal with the land. I agreed not to interfere with natural processes.

"But since you were the one who created it, you could interfere as you wish. I ask you: Help him.

Jesus, unshaven and dressed in jeans and a striped T-shirt, made a serious face, analyzing the situation for a moment. Then he concluded:

"It's ok. What don't I do for you?

That said, the creator flew in all his glory from his throne towards Earth. When he got very close, he exclaimed:

"Earth, why are you tormenting him?

"I am tormenting him because he refuses to fulfill my wishes: I want him to breed.

"It's no use. He is a very evolved spirit. It will not give in to your temptations.

"I do not want to know. For me, he is just like anyone.

"Don't torment him anymore. I am sending you. Obey.

"Why would you obey?

"Because I raised you.

"I don't remember being raised. I just know that I came out of a big explosion.

"I was the one who teased her.

"Right. But you must know by natural law that no spirit can interfere in matter. So, I will continue to torment you.

"If you continue, I will destroy you.

"If you destroy me, you will also destroy all of his creation.

This response from Earth made Jesus reflect. Indeed, this was a great truth, and as he loved humanity infinitely, he stopped insisting. Then he returned to heaven, found his mother and comforted her:

"I haven't been able to do it yet. But do not worry. I will think of something to help you.

"Yes, I trust. This young man will still be pleased. (She replied)

23.2-God's proposal

It had been eight months since Divine had finished her electrical engineering course and her life continued as monotonous as ever. Of novelty, only completion in the basic computer course. However, no work proposal had appeared.

While he did not reach his goals, he continued his studies for the competition as usual in the morning and in the afternoon, it was the time for leisure. One of those afternoons, he took the opportunity to meditate on life and its implications: Death, time, future, end. In this exercise, he received a visit from the breeder who promptly communicated with him:

"Are you afraid of death, Divine? Know that death does not exist because you are an eternal being.

"I know I am. But this is not enough to control the feeling that invades me when I think of it: Knowing that everything I built and struggled with will be lost with my memory.

"You won't get lost. You will live through your writings. Have you thought about the number of people you will help? Their memory will not be erased for them. Remember: if there were no death there would be no life and vice versa.

These words moved Divine a lot, and he started to cry compulsively. God then intervened:

"Why are you crying? Don't cry if I'm not going to cry either.

"I cannot explain. It is involuntary.

"What you want? Do you want me to do the same thing to you as I did to Henoch?

"How would it be?

"I would trigger a hurricane and take you to the living skies. Every day, I go back to earth to get food for him. He's beautiful like you.

"No, thank you. I am no better than my parents. I have to fulfill my mission. Besides, I would die if I went into a hurricane.

"I would not die, man of little faith. You would not lose a single strand of your hair.

Something compelled Divine to continue crying inconsolably. God then again intervened:

"Stop it, spoiled young man. Look, I promise you will be the first to be resurrected in the new world. Did you know that so far, the angels are crying?

"Forgive me. I am a fool. When will the new world arrive?

"Ten a thousand years from now. If you reveal this secret, there is no problem. I change my plans.

"Do not worry. I know how to keep secrets when necessary. Thank you for the words.

"You're welcome. Well, I'll be right there. When you die, I will come and get you. Rather, I want to reveal a mystery to you: You are one of the small particles of the Risen Christ. In my immense kindness, I wanted my son to be eternal. So, I turned its sacred particles into spirits. You are one of them, the most blessed. I find my pleasure in you. Isn't it surprising? While the world will mourn your loss, I will smile, for you, will return to my home.

That said, the divine spirit has definitely moved away leaving Divine alone. Then tranquility reigned again.

23.3-Gabriel's coming

It was dawn.

A new day was beginning and Divine was ready (body and soul) to face him. His spiritual guide warned him: A compelling God is approaching. What does he want with you?

When he got closer, Gabriel descended into his room with his shiny wings and started the conversation with Divine's angel:

"Do you mean to say that this is the man God chose to spread his message and bring people closer to the light? Is gorgeous.

"Yes, is this. It is the most beautiful of all that he chose over time (more inside than outside). (Angel)

"So fragile and so unprotected. Is he prepared to shoulder the responsibilities of his mission?

"Of course, it is. God does not make mistakes. With my help, he will have a bright future.

"If you need help, just call me. I'll be attentive.

"Thanks. We will call yes.

Gabriel greeted the angel of the order and blessed Divine. Then he started flapping his long wings and finally walked away. It had been an incredible experience for both parties.

23.4-A new chance

Destruction bar

At approximately 1:00 am, the party that had started two hours ago was still hectic: young couples dating, countless dancing couples, some were drugged and others were passed out on the floor (Overcome by the effect of alcohol).

Among these were Gilbert (a young man full of life, dreams, and expectations) accompanied by some colleagues. They rested at a table after an intense round of drinks, food, and dancing.

Until at some point a girl attracted his attention and as he was touched by the drink, he decided to invest in it. He got up from the table, came to the girl, took her by the hips and said:

"How about going out with me?

"What is this, man? Are you crazy? I am committed.

"You're lying. Nobody would leave a beauty like you alone.

"We'd better stop here. Leave me alone.

Oblivious to everyone and her requests, Gilbert did not care. He kissed her forcefully, took her arm and started to lead her out of the bar. Desperate, the girl who was called Cristina, started screaming for help.

Her attitude caught the attention of those present, including that of her boyfriend, Eduardo, who was a little distant. When he realized what was happening to his beloved, he was furious and left to defend her.

When he got close to the two, with incredible agility, he freed the girl from the brazen and went into a hand-to-hand fight with Gilbert. As he was sober, he took advantage and, at the right moment, pulled a dagger from his waist that he always carried. Without pity, he stuck in the opponent's heart. It was enough to immobilize him.

At this point, the others intruded. They put the fight aside, but it was too late. The blow had been deadly and Gilbert had died on the spot. They only had the job of carrying it and taking it home.

Meanwhile, his spirit began to wander. He found his angel, but he was not aware of what had happened. Due to fate, he and his angel approached Divine. The same can hear and feel the heated debate between them:

"You already passed away. (Guardian)

"I am alive. Cannot you see me? (Gilbert)

"You are just a spirit. Your place now is the spiritual plane. Come with me! (Guardian)

"I do not accept. I was just a young man of eighteen. I wanted to love, walk and have children. Anyway, live. (Gilbert)

"You have to conform. What is done is no longer to be done. (guardian)

"I wanted a new chance. Go back to live. I promise to be a better person. I want to take new actions and give more value to the miracle that is life.

Now, emotion was taking over him and everyone present. Divine then moaned and cried out:

"Dad, give it another chance. May he be born again and be able to accomplish everything he has not accomplished in this life.

Right after this request, a light shone brightly around them leaving Gilbert impressed:

"What light is that? (He asked)

"It is the creator. He heard this angel's prayer. Your memories will almost all be erased, and you will be born again. (Informed the guardian)

Moved, he moved closer to Divine and in a farewell tone said:

"Thanks for existing. I will never forget what you did for me.

That said, he went away with his angel towards the light. There, a new cycle of reincarnations would begin, provided instantly by Divine's prayer.

Meanwhile, the backwoods bud would continue its saga on Earth searching for its destiny. Let's move forward!

23.5-The encounter with the Devil

Life went on. Even without understanding, with the experiences he lived, Divine encompassed a more significant amount of information about the existing dimensions, preparing him for the mission that was beginning.

Although his role was unclear, he understood that he had been chosen from among many for success, achievement and eternal discovery. It was up to him to pass this on in some way to the universe that welcomed him and that was too late. But this was something for the future.

For now, the moment was one of discoveries. One of them that was a watershed was the encounter with the black archangel.

This episode took place in a secret place, spacious, wide, with little lighting and at the moment Divine was completely alone. This place is on the border between the two worlds.

That was when the tempter approached and the dialogue started:

"Who are you? (Asked Divine)

"I am known as the Devil.

"What do you want with me?

"I come to make you a proposal. Stay by my side and I will give you the world in return.

"Because you want me? I am a weak and powerless man.

"Do not depreciate yourself. You have a lot of value.

"Know. But at the moment I am not interested in the proposal.

"He is sure? What if I get angry? Aren't you afraid of me?

"Why would it be?

"I am a monster with seven wings and three horns.

"I'm seeing. However, I am not impressed.

"I could dominate you.

"If you did that, I would die of boredom because my life is dull and full of suffering.

"This is just a phase. The boom will follow. Are you sure you don't want to think about my proposal?

"No. I simply do not serve your kingdom because I am good.

"I understand. We are then enemies. Even so, I admire your effort and dedication.

"Thanks. Look, I have a question. Could you get me out?

"It depends. What do you want to know?

"Are you an angel or a brother of God?

"What I can tell you are that I am all that is bad in the world. Neither you nor anyone can really know who I am. If I knew, I would die. Something more?

"No. Thanks.

"Goodbye. We'll still see each other.

That said, he finally walked away, disappearing from the scene. The son of God was left alone. Soon after, Divine transported herself back to her home. I was to be congratulated for resisting. Let's continue!

23.6-The city of men

Another important moment in the life of Divine, who was already twenty years old, was the discovery of the secret of the seven doors. With this new asset in hand, he had accessed several times to a spiritual plane very close to ours known as "City of men".

In this illuminated place with characteristics close to our planet, he discovered an evolved humanity, but still with material remnants. Everyone who lived there had needs for food, physiological and even sex.

This period was very productive, but he ended up giving it up because he was willing to live his normal life without much absorption. It was not yet time to delve into these issues.

The central issue was on earth and would focus on it alone. Then he said goodbye to the "City of men" once and for all. It was traumatic, but extremely necessary for his mental health.

Life goes on!

23.7- The fisherman

Tired of the monotony and routine that had transformed his life, Divine decided to go for a walk promoted in his community. The destination was the beach and with some effort, her mother agreed to pay for her ticket.

With everything combined, on the scheduled day and time, the minibus departed from Leaf Village. Crossing some streets, he took the BR 232 lane and headed towards Recife. In approximately three hours of travel, he had the unique opportunity to pass through a range of cities that he had never imagined. More proof that life was not limited to its stronghold.

They entered the capital and went to the beach for a good trip. Faced with congested traffic, it took another hour until the disembarkation near the destination. Finally, they got out of the car.

Together with his colleagues, Divine began to play in the sand. He stayed in this exercise for a while. Then he went away to drink coconut water near the beach. It was on this occasion that the presence of a short, thick, old white man, with black hair and good looks caught his attention. He decided to get closer. When he got very close, the man noticed and shouted:

"Son of God, what are you doing here?

"You know me? Why do you ask for explanations of something that does not concern you?

Despite Divine's unpleasant comment, the man didn't seem to care. So much so that he walked a little further and when he got to his side, he resumed the conversation with a serious air.

"A thousand pardons, but it is that I perceived the suffering and anguish in your heart. Can I help you with anything?

Strangely Divine felt total confidence in that man. So, she decided to tell him a little about her troubled life.

"Yes, at least listening. Look, I have visions, dreams, foreboding, and intuitions. I see in them a little of the present, past, and future. Despite that, I don't understand why it comes in the form of riddles. Do I see the future? I see, but I can't help it. Do I see the past? I see. Memories are worthless.

"Don't deny your gifts. They make them special. Use them for good because your path is light. Don't care what others think.

"I have so many doubts when I'm at the bottom of the well: No job, no friends, no strength to keep fighting. In addition, I have had visions that have not yet come to pass.

"Everything has its time, boy. The storm at some point will pass reaching the calm. Have faith in God. He loves you infinitely and will never abandon you. Remember: Among all human beings, you are the only one who has no reason to doubt him because he gave you countless proofs of the splendid future, he planned for you.

"Yes, I know. I know this plan. All of this further increases my responsibility in the journey of my life.

"Well, now I have to go. I will prepare these fish that I caught.

"Go in peace, my brother and thank you.

"You're welcome.

That said, he started to walk away. However, being at a medium distance, he turned back and exclaimed:

"May you accomplish everything in your life!

Then he continued on his usual path, disappearing moments later. Divine then returned with his colleagues and for the rest of the day he enjoyed the tour without comment on what had happened.

At the end of the day, they returned to the bus, starting the way back. At the scheduled time, they arrived home normally and Divine took the opportunity to rest a lot. What was going to happen? Keep following, readers!

24-The three-year period (2004-2006)

After the mysterious encounter with the fisherman, Divine returned to his usual activities without any major concerns. Life went on normally. Within three years, some relevant facts happened. The main ones were: New approvals in public and entrance exams, beginning of work in literature as therapy, thus emerging his first book, existential and nervous crisis and sinking into the dark night of the soul.

In this happy, sad, troubled and complicated period at the same time, he had the support of his family and closest friends, counting on everyone's patience. He was twenty-three years old, and he felt indebted to everyone.

Now it was time to move on with my studies, other activities and work as I expected to be called soon. Onward, warrior! We are with you.

25-New cycle

2007 begins. Early on, good news: Divine had received a letter inviting him to present documents and medical exams in the competition he had passed. Immediately, the same thing was to take care of the details and after fifteen days, everything was ready.

And there he went. He traveled about 40 km (forty kilometers), took possession and agreed on the details of the contract. It would start the other week, and it would be his first work experience earning a minimum wage.

It was a first step even with all the difficulties involved: Distance, low salary, inexperience, fear, and the possibility of reconciling with the college that started in a federal institution that promised to be demanding.

Furthermore, it was also something new, and he felt it was the right time to change some air, meet new people, get distracted, stifle his gift that still bothered him and live without fear of being happy as the song says.

He was willing to show the world his potential, to be proud of the Towers like the legendary Victor and Rafael, to have the long-awaited "Meeting between two worlds" that would make his destiny a little clearer and more peaceful.

I would try again without fear of the consequences. Whatever God wanted! Good luck, Divine.

26-Beginning of work and classes

A new life was beginning for Divine with the beginning of work concurrently with college classes. Two of your achievements. At work, he was allocated in the financial part of the city hall and was very well-received by co-workers, both new and old. In a few days he demonstrated his potential and was already praised by him. As a first experience, all his efforts were worthwhile.

At school, in addition to the unique opportunity to deepen his studies and complete his higher education (parents' dream), the situation provided him with the interaction with more than forty-nine different people. The day-to-day constructions were wealthy and there was no way that the room could be said to be ordinary.

Divine's life was progressing gradually with improvements in every way and the prospects were not the worst. Fortunately! Divine deserved for all his effort. But nothing was yet defined.

Two months later, the circumstances that followed led Divine to make a serious new decision: Quit her job. It wouldn't be this time that he would help his family. The reasons for this oscillated between lack of control of the gift, persistent nervous crisis, impossibility to reconcile with studies and the biggest one (although he did not admit it) was an overwhelming passion that consumed him and that he had no hope of being reciprocated. Once again, she ran away from love without even trying. Do not repeat this mistake, readers! Fight for your happiness.

Now his focus was only on studies once again and everyone at home understood and supported him. At least he hoped to control his instincts and not fall back into the trap of the dark night that he didn't even want to remember. Cruel times those!

A new "crossing" started for the modern towers.

27-Important facts in four years (2007-2010)

27.1-The stigmatized book

Even in the first semester of college, Divine had contact with a couple, two figures who stood out among colleagues. Once, in a group work, a debate about religion started and with the experience, that the young man mentioned was one of the most active.

It is not known why, but they realized their naivety and in a private conversation they offered help. They promised to bring you something that would clear up your doubts. Without realizing the evil, Divine accepted.

The other day, they fulfilled their promise and at the end of class they gave him the book. In a nutshell, they explained that it was special and that it would be of great help to clarify certain facts. However, they warned that there was danger in staying with him for more than a day. The carrier could even die. Although intrigued, Divine accepted him and took him home.

When he arrived, he read a few pages and each line was more astonished by the secrets he revealed. That book really was wonderful! After a few hours, he got tired and went to bed with the book on the side and hoped to have the dream of the Gods deserved. However, he found the opposite.

In a tormented night, he lived close to the horrors of a war that involved billions of lives. How much pain, suffering, hatred, for an unjust but necessary cause. It was like I was there with them, all the time and there was nothing I could do.

So, the worst night of his life went on, surrounded by shadows, light, screams, and blood. When I woke up, it was destroyed. With great effort, he got up, cursed the couple and their attitude in accepting the loan. It was not cool to act that way.

In the morning and afternoon, he took care of his normal activities involving studies, housework, listening to music, reading a book, watching TV, taking a walk, going to the library, chatting, etc. At all times, I thought of nothing else but the cursed, stigmatized book, and he, as a sensitive medium, could not read at all. He was determined not to repeat the experience ever again.

In the evening, after the bath, he went to college taking the book with him. Do not leave your memory that you could not stay with him for more than a day. Otherwise, death was likely.

He arrived around 7:00 pm, entered room 6 on the second block and sat in one of the front chairs as usual. The other colleagues gradually arrived and the couple had not yet arrived. Fifteen minutes later, classes started.

Time passed and to Divine's despair the sayings that did not appear. Towards the end of the class, her only way out was to ask for help from her great friend who always sat beside her.

She explained the situation in detail, and luckily, she accepted the book for her home, freeing him from the curse. At least he had saved time thanks to that formidable girl.

The other day, the two came and finally the book was returned to the owners from where it should never have left. Shortly afterwards, they left the course and their destination is not known. What Divine knew was that he had experienced a strange force due to both and that he would never forget. Get lost, stigmatized book! Never! So, I hoped.

Life that follows.

27.2-The dream of literature

As I said earlier, Divine had completed his first handwritten book. Due to the few conditions, I had, the only way out was to type it in at work in the hours of the break. He did this for a month resulting in a total of 37 pages.

Without much knowledge and guidance, he registered it at the registry office at an exorbitant price when the correct thing would be to register it at the national library in Rio de Janeiro or at the state post.

The next step was to send it to a publisher. And it did. He sent it to a major Catholic-themed publisher when the subject of the book was somewhat linked to the spirits part containing dreams, sonnets, essays and phrases of wisdom.

Three months later the answer: Failed. It was a shock to his pretensions, causing him to become demotivated a little. He decided to stop writing even though he knew he had a lot of talent. The dream was not yet within reach.

27.3- New challenges

The year 2008 begins. During this period, Divine Torres continued with his usual dedication to his daily study, leisure and social activities. However, his reality of poverty and loneliness persisted with his whole family and this was something that bothered him a lot.

At the end of the same year, a light at the end of the tunnel began to emerge: Approvals in two public offices with workplaces close to his residence. It looked like the situation was finally going to change after a lot of fighting.

While he was not called, he took advantage of his free time to engage in reading, outings with friends and parties. Life had to be lived!

27.4-2009

From the beginning, 2009 presented itself as a decisive year in the life of Victor Torres' grandson, Divine. Among the achievements, the call for the position of administrative assistant in the neighboring city hall and the resumption of his dream of literature, starting to write a new book.

Three months later, in May, he had already adapted to the work and finished the book, 148 pages in total. However, he decided to keep it for a while because he still didn't have enough money to buy a computer to type it in.

The dream of literature was for later. The current moment was dedicated exclusively to work and to the faculty of Mathematics, which was very demanding. I was already in the fifth period without pending in any discipline thanks to your efforts.

As for the question of spirituality, it was more controlled and developed than ever. With his vision of the future, he already knew that he would be a federal servant and that he would have the success he deserved in literature. This fueled his dreams of conquering the world!

Let's move forward.

27.5-The last year of college

2010 started out promising for the Torres. Another call to assume another public position (state) and Divine left the city hall. Immediately, I was starting the seventh term of college with many proprieties.

The financial situation would improve a little with him starting to help with household expenses and this was excellent. Although it was not the ideal position, he would cover his monthly expenses smoothly.

About the heart, the situation was the same: Always alone. But he didn't care. I was still young and the possibilities were very great. Whatever had to would be, on time and at the right time!

Towards the end of the year, his life became busier: Several trips and elaboration of the course conclusion work. All very fast and well-used.

Luckily, everything worked out, and he finally finished his studies. He was the first graduate of the entire family. Pride for your mother. From that day on, I expected only success after many struggles, deprivations, obstacles overcome and a lot of pain. But he had survived for his faith, for having seer blood and for being the descendant of the legendary Victor, a great man from the Northeast.

Onward, Divine!

28-Current weather

The predictions were being made little by little in his life in the next three and a half years. He became a published writer, became a federal employee and loved several times having interesting experiences.

This new reality has made it possible to have greater control over your gift, greater social contact, new friendships and with the money, you have earned you can be more helpful to those in need. In short, he had been reborn as a man and had transformed the lives of everyone around him. He had made the Torres proud and would always continue to fight for his dreams. Do this too, readers! No matter the difficulties, the stereotypes, the prejudices, never be discouraged! Despite not having conquered everything yet, Divine is an inspiring example because he never stopped believing that it was possible to transform his reality.

"If you want to be universal, start by painting your village". (Leon Tolstoy)

End of vision

29-Back to the room

The co-vision is gone. Renato and I woke up from the trance and exhausted we sat on the floor. The healer waits for a few seconds and then helps us to get up. With a signal, we left the room and settled on stools in what would be the hut room.

We face each other to face each other and with an air of curiosity the master starts the conversation:

"What's up? Was the experience fruitful?

"Excellent. Divine's story inspired me to continue fighting for my dreams. (Observed Renato)

"Rescuing this story was important to me. It took me to a deep reflection and in the end, I conclude that I have a little Divine and Victor in me too. I am already a winner despite everything. (The seer)

"Very well. This was the goal. I am certain that from now on, they will continue their lives with more courage, strength, and faith than usual. I wish you both successes. My part is done. (Healer)

"I would like to thank you for all your dedication and commitment to our cause. Thanks. (Renato)

"Idem. We will never forget the Lord! (The seer)

At this moment tears dried up with suffering came down on the master's face. Never in his life had he felt so loved. If I died at this moment, I would go in peace.

"Thank you, friends. I will not forget you, either. Good luck and goodbye. (Healer)

The three approaches and greeted each other with a triple hug. At the end of the hug, they finally left. Outside, they took the dirt road that would take them to the edge of the Highway again. Now, back home, after so long.

30-At home

The trip went smoothly. Renato was handed over to the guardian and the seer found his family in peace again. After missing him, he returned to his usual jobs.

As long as I didn't have the opportunity for another adventure, I would enjoy such important family moments. Thus, this third stage ended with the awareness of mission accomplished. He was just a little saddened by the news of the death of his two masters: Angel and a healer.

Well, I had to settle for these facts. They should have already accomplished their mission. Now it remained to continue the path of the seer who promised to be long and challenging with his assistant Renato. Let new adventures come then!

Conclusion

Having exposed the facts, we realize how important it is to believe in our values, ideals, and our faith, whatever it may be. Directed by them and taking concrete actions, we can finally achieve particular victories at every step. And it's not just in fiction! We have countless examples in this country of winning people and groups that started practically from scratch.

My personal advice: Invest in your potential without measuring efforts that the destiny will show for you. It is not necessary to be super. hero or psychic like the characters in the book to get exactly where you want. It only takes planning and intelligence to choose the shortest path to success.

I sincerely hope that everyone who reads this book will feel inspired, go out to fight and achieve the happiness and success they deserve. Hugs, a loving kiss and see you next time.

The author

END

9 786599 447396